Feast with the
King

FRANCESCA SIMON
Illustrated by Steve May

faber

For my opera mentors —
John Fulljames and Kasper Holten.
F. S.

For Jackie & Andy for all the support and enthusiasm!
S. M.

First published in 2023 by
Faber & Faber Limited
Bloomsbury House, 74–77 Great Russell Street,
London WC1B 3DA
faber.co.uk
and
Profile Books
29 Cloth Fair, London EC1A 7JQ
profilebooks.com

Typeset in Sweater School by MRules
This font has been specially chosen to support reading
Printed by CPI Group (UK) Ltd, Croydon CR0 4YY

A CIP record for this book is available from the British Library

ISBN 978–0–571–34953–1

MIX
Paper | Supporting
responsible forestry
FSC® C171272

Printed and bound in the UK on FSC paper in line with our continuing
commitment to ethical business practices, sustainability and the environment.
For further information see faber.co.uk/environmental-policy

2 4 6 8 10 9 7 5 3 1

Contents

Characters

Hack  Whack

Bitey-Bitey

Twisty Pants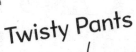

Dirty Ulf

Elsa Gold-Hair

HACK AND WHACK BABYSIT FIRE HAZARD

'On your guard!' shrieked Hack, waving her sword.

'On **your** guard!' shrieked Whack, swinging his axe.

Smash! Crash!

1

Wooden platters, knives and antler spoons clattered to the dirt floor.

'Is this how you grind the wheat, Hack?' said Mum, dashing in from the storeroom.

Her hands were covered in bread dough. 'Whack! Where's that chicken I told you to pluck? The herrings need gutting. The milk needs churning. You're the worst Vikings in the village. Now put down those weapons and do your chores, or no dinner tonight.'

Hack sighed loudly and stomped over to the bread trough. She hated grinding wheat. It took FOREVER and no matter how long she turned the quern stone to crush the grain there was always so much grit in the flour. Ugh. Bread made from gritty flour tasted horrible. It was amazing she still had teeth.

I might as well scoop up dirt from the floor and eat that, thought Hack. When she grew up, she'd make sure she had loads of servants to do all the chores. **She'd** go raiding and bring back so much gold and silver that she would never have to lift a finger again and she could spend all day playing and sword-fighting.

Outside, the sun was actually shining. It was awful being stuck indoors.

Whack stomped over to the table and glared at the chicken he was supposed to be plucking.

Why was he inside on such a nice day? He wanted to be outside chasing goats off the roof and running in the woods with his wolf cub Bitey-Bitey.

Hack started grinding the wheat.

Whack started plucking the chicken.

Mum glared at them, then got on with her bread-making. 'And no dawdling!' she shouted.

'Quick, let's get out of here,' hissed Whack.

'Yeah,' said Hack.

The terrible twins tiptoed to the door. Whack was just about to open it when Dirty Ulf's mum burst into their longhouse, without even waiting for someone to let her in.

'I've got to go up to the summer pastures,' said Dirty Ulf's mother, red-faced and panting. 'Dirty Ulf is already there. Can you two babysit Fire Hazard till night-meal?'

Look after Fire Hazard instead of grinding wheat and plucking chickens?

'We'll do it,' said Hack and Whack. What a brilliant way to get out of doing their chores. How hard could it be to watch a two-year-old for a few hours?

'You want Hack and Whack . . . to **babysit**?' said Mum.

'Yup,' said Dirty Ulf's mother, racing out the door. 'What's the worst that can happen?' she shouted over her shoulder, as she ran towards the mountains.

Fire Hazard was Dirty Ulf's little brother. He was always smiling and laughing, but he loved playing with kindling and starting fires.

'Bye, Mum,' shouted Hack.

'C'mon, Bitey-Bitey,' said Whack, as they skipped over to Dirty Ulf's. Her messy longhouse was smaller than theirs, but it smelled just the same — of turf and smoke and dung and fish oil. Clothes, shoes, fishing nets and sheepskins were scattered everywhere.

Fire Hazard was standing on the worn wooden table, waving around some kindling.

'Fire,' he beamed. 'Fire!'

'Hi, Fire Hazard,' said Hack.

'Nice kindling,' said Whack.

'Let's see what food they've got,' said Hack.

'We can do whatever we want,' said Whack.

'Fire,' shouted Fire Hazard, whirling around on the table. 'Fire!'

Hack peered inside a storage barrel.

'Ooh, strawberries,' she said, scooping up a handful.

'And raspberries,' said Whack, helping himself.

'This is the life,' said Hack, munching and crunching.

'Fire,' said Fire Hazard, waddling over to the hearth and picking up more kindling. 'Fire!'

he shouted.

Hack lifted the lid on another barrel.

'Honey cakes,' she said. 'Dirty Ulf kept that quiet.'

'Gimme some,' said Whack.

'I love honey cakes,' said Hack, gorging on as many as she could cram into her mouth at once.

Whack grabbed a handful of honey cakes and stuffed them into his mouth.

Fire Hazard tried to set fire to the table.

'Oh yum, nuts,' said Whack.

Fire Hazard tried to set fire to a bucket.

'Let's see what they've got in their storage chest,' said Whack.

Fire Hazard tried to set fire to Bitey-Bitey's tail.

'Look at these cloaks,' said Hack, trying one on. 'I'm the queen of the world,' she shouted, parading up and down, the long

cloak dragging on the floor. 'On your knees, thrall,' she ordered, twirling her sword.

'And fur hats,' said Whack, piling two on his head. 'I'm the king! I rule that everyone has to give me their gold arm rings or lose their heads.'

Fire Hazard tried to set fire to the wooden toilet seat.

'I order you to—' Hack sniffed. 'Do you smell something?'

'Just you,' said Whack, grabbing a cloak. 'You smell like a rotten herring.'

'Ha! You smell like a dead seal,' said Hack, pushing Whack.

Whack pushed her back.

'Stink face!'

'Whale blubber!'

'I think I smell burning,' said Hack.

Whack stopped prancing. 'Me too,' he said.

'Fire!' beamed Fire Hazard, setting fire to the loom.

'Not the loom, Fire Hazard,' said Whack.

'Put that stick back in the hearth, Fire Hazard,' said Hack.

Fire Hazard ignored them.

'Fire!' he said, waving around the sticks.

There was now a big, burnt hole in the cloth stretched on the loom.

'Do you think anyone will notice?' said Hack.

'Nah,' said Whack.

'We need to distract him,' said Hack. 'Come over here, Fire Hazard. I've got a really fun plan. Let's surprise your mummy when she gets back with how many new words you can say.'

'Fire!' said Fire Hazard.

'You can't just keep saying **fire**,' said Whack.

'Now repeat after me,' said Hack. 'Troll.'

'Troll,' said Fire Hazard.

'See, you can do it,' said Whack.

'Stinky troll,' said Hack.

'Stinky troll,' said Fire Hazard.

'Squelchy belchy belly,' said Hack.

'Squelchy belchy belly,' said Fire Hazard, pointing to his round tummy.

'Good job,' said Hack. 'Now say, "Mum has a squelchy belchy troll belly".'

'Mum has a squelchy belchy troll belly,' said Fire Hazard, laughing.

'She'll be so pleased when you tell her,' said Hack.

'Now say, "Rumbly bumbly bottom",' said Whack.

'Rumbly bumbly bottom,' said Fire Hazard.

'Dad has a rumbly bumbly bottom,' said Whack.

'Dad has a rumbly bumbly bottom,' repeated Fire Hazard.

'Bogey bum bum,' said Hack.

'Bogey bum bum,' said Fire Hazard.

'Bogey bum bum bum BUM!' chanted Hack and Whack.

'BOGEY BUM BUM BUM BUM!' repeated Fire Hazard, toddling off to the storeroom.

'I'm exhausted,' said Hack.

'It's hard work looking after a toddler,' said Whack.

THUNK! THUD! GLUG GLUG GLUG SPLASH!

SPLASH!

'What was that?' said Hack.

'Sounds like water spilling,' said Whack.

Hack and Whack ran into the storeroom.

SQUELCH!

SQUELCH!

SQUELCH!

There were puddles and overturned barrels everywhere.

'Oops,' said Whack.

'Beer,' sang Fire Hazard,

23

splashing in the puddles.

Hack and Whack watched him stomping and splashing.

'Oh well, let him have his fun,' said Hack.

'Hack! Whack! Come on out, we're playing ball,' shouted Twisty Pants. 'We need some more players.'

Hack looked at Whack.

Whack looked at Hack.

They loved playing ball.

'Give Fire Hazard something

to play with,' said Hack.

'Here, Fire Hazard, you can play with this axe,' said Whack.

'Axe!' said Fire Hazard, beaming.

'C'mon, let's go,' said Whack.

The terrible twins dropped their borrowed cloaks and hats in the beer puddles and ran out into the sunshine.

'I'm captain!' shouted Hack.

'I'm captain!' shouted Whack.

'I'm captain!' shouted Scar Leg.

'It's my ball, and if I'm not captain I won't play,' said Twisty Pants.

'But it's **my** bat,' said Loud Mouth, swinging it.

'You can't be captain, Loud Mouth – you're a terrible player,' said Whack.

'Am not,' said Loud Mouth.

'Are too,' said Whack.

'Luckily I'm the best player who's ever lived,' bragged Twisty Pants.

'Better than Valgard the Slayer?' said Hack.

Valgard the Slayer had killed everyone on the opposite team, then claimed victory.

'Much better,' said Twisty Pants.

'But you've never played before, Twisty Pants,' said Black Tooth.

'So?' said Twisty Pants. 'I don't have to play to know **I'm** the best.'

'But none of you ever follows the rules!' wailed Elsa Gold-Hair. She hated ball games. They always ended with everyone fighting and shouting.

'I'm captain!' shouted Hack.

'I'm captain!' shouted Whack. 'Now hand over the bat.'

'Who's gonna make me?' snarled Loud Mouth.

'We are!' shouted Hack and Whack.

Hack drew her sword.

Whack drew his axe.

Loud Mouth handed over the bat and the game began.

'You cheated, Scar Leg!' screamed Little Sparrow.

'You dropped the ball and

picked it up!' shouted Black Tooth.

'Didn't,' said Scar Leg.

'Did!'

'My ball went over the goal line,' said Scar Leg.

'No way! I stopped it,' said Black Tooth.

'FOUR people can't tackle the person who caught the ball,' said Elsa. 'Only ONE!'

'Those aren't the rules,' said Twisty Pants. 'If you trip and lose the ball, you have to run backwards.'

'Not a chance, Twisty Pants,' shouted Spear Nose. 'You only have to run backwards if you trip **before** you catch the ball.'

'That's pig poo,' said Twisty Pants.

'That's the rule,' said Spear Nose.

'Cheater,' snarled Loud Mouth.

'**You're** the cheater,' snarled Hack.

Loud Mouth glared at Hack.

They both drew their swords

when –

MOO!

MOO!

MOOOOOOO!

A herd of cows stampeded through the playing field, then ran down the hill towards the sea. The two teams tumbled out of the way of the pounding hooves.

'Those are my cows!' yelped Little Sparrow.

'And mine!' yelped Scar Leg.

'And mine!' shouted Elsa Gold-Hair.

'Help! Help! Cows on the loose!' they screamed, racing after the disappearing herd.

SQUAWK! SQUAWK!

SQUAWK!

A huge flock of cackling chickens pelted past, chased by a screeching Pecky-Pecky — the meanest hen in the village.

'My chickens!' yelled Twisty Pants.

'Who let them out?' yelled Red Cheek.

OINK! OINK! OINK!

'Pigs! Watch out!' shouted Black Tooth. The pigs galloped into the woods, chased by Thrain Scatter-Brain and his wife Gyda the Proud.

'Just wait till I catch who let my pigs out! I'll banish them to Greenland,' shrieked Thrain.

'After I've stuffed Hack and Whack into a barrel of rotten herrings!' shrieked Gyda.

'But it wasn't us!' shouted Whack.

'But if it wasn't us,' said Hack, 'then who was it? **We're** the worst Vikings in the village ...'

Hack looked at Whack.

Whack looked at Hack.

'You don't think ...'

'No way ...'

Hack and Whack raced back
to Dirty Ulf's longhouse.

Embers were smouldering

everywhere. Spoons and pitchers and drinking horns lay scattered on the floor. Storage barrels were tipped over. Ripped cushions and balls of wool lay unravelled in beer puddles. Benches and buckets were overturned. An axe stuck out of a stool.

Fire Hazard was GONE.

'We'd better find him,' said Hack. 'C'mon, Bitey-Bitey – find Fire Hazard.'

'Awhoooooo awhooooooo awhoooooooooooooo,' howled Bitey-Bitey, curling up on a torn cloak in front of the hearth fire and scratching his fleas. Which, in Wolf, meant, 'I would rather bite my own backside than help you find that horrible human.'

Hack and Whack ran through the village following the trail of smoking fires, burning bread, knocked-down woodpiles, upside-down bread troughs, scattered fish and open gates. All around them people were running about and shouting.

'My storehouse is on fire!'

'My boar is out of the home meadow!'

'My toilet is upside down!'

'Look,' shouted Elsa Gold-Hair. 'The boats! Someone's untied all the boats!'

Hack and Whack ran down to the shore, climbing over piles of logs and overturned barrels.

Boats bobbed in the harbour, cut loose from their moorings.

Fire Hazard was stomping in the shallow waves, trying to set them on fire, clapping and laughing.

'Fire Hazard!' shouted Hack. 'Just for today you're the worst Viking in the village. Time to come home.'

Fire Hazard stood on the beach with his arms folded and shook his head.

'We can light a fire ...' said Whack.

'Fire!' said Fire Hazard, trotting after them.

Glumra Bug-Bear was piling up all the fallen logs from her woodpile.

'Stinky troll,' said Fire Hazard, pointing at Glumra Bug-Bear.

Glumra gasped. '**What** did you say?'

'Squelchy belchy belly,' said Fire Hazard.

Eystein Smelly Fart was picking up all the dried fish

scattered across his yard.

'Bogey bum bum,' chortled Fire Hazard, pointing.

'Rumbly bumbly bottom,' shrieked Fire Hazard, pointing at Hildi Horn-Head.

'Troll face!' he yelled at Bragi Bread-Nose.

'Wobbly bobbly smelly belly,' he screeched at Sven Fork-Beard.

'Bogey bum bum bum BUM!' he trilled at Erik Gold-Hair.

'Fire Hazard, that's very naughty,' said Hack loudly.

'We're just the babysitters,' said Whack.

'I blame the parents,' said Hack.

Hack and Whack picked up a few dried fish. They put the storage barrels upright. They stomped on the fires. They righted the loom and hid the torn and burnt cloth. There were leeks and berries scattered all over the floor, clothes spilling out of chests, broken drinking horns and beer puddles everywhere. Despite all their hard work, the longhouse still looked like a herd of wild pigs had rampaged through it.

'I'm exhausted,' said Hack.

'I've never worked so hard in my life,' said Whack.

'Fire,' said Fire Hazard, beaming.

'We're going to be in big trouble when his mum gets home,' said Hack.

'What do we do?' said Whack.

'Let's tell her trolls attacked,' said Hack.

'And that we fought them off,'

said Whack.

'But then a herd of wild pigs ran in,' said Hack.

'And ogres,' said Whack.

'Three of them,' said Hack.

'Three of what?' said Dirty Ulf's mother, walking through the door.

'That's how many ogres we fought today,' said Whack. 'When they attacked us and messed up the place.'

'What mess?' said Dirty Ulf's mother, sitting down on a stool and yawning. 'Ooof, I'm tired,' she said, untying her boots and rubbing her feet. 'What a day.'

'Fire!' said Fire Hazard, running over to her.

'Hello, piglet,' said his mother. 'Thanks, Hack and Whack — you two are **great** babysitters!'

'We are?' said Whack.

'Really?' said Hack.

'He's alive, isn't he?' said Dirty

Ulf's mother. 'Can you come again tomorrow?'

Look after Fire Hazard **again**?

'Uhh, sorry, I have to gut fish,' said Whack.

'Sorry, I have to churn butter,' said Hack.

'Mum has a squelchy belchy stinky troll belly,' said Fire Hazard.

'Bye,' shouted Hack and Whack, racing out the door and into a crowd of angry Vikings marching towards Dirty Ulf's longhouse.

'He's the worst Viking in the village today,' said Hack.

'But tomorrow ... watch out!' shouted Whack.

HACK AND WHACK FEAST WITH THE KING

The king was coming to Bear Island! The chieftain Thrain Scatter-Brain had heard the exciting news from Olga Fish-Belly's uncle's nephew's cousin's aunt's son, who'd met some sailors in the king's army while he'd been raiding over the summer.

King Leif the Very Uptight, son of King Leif the Uptight, was coming to Bear Island. He'd be arriving just after the new moon. There was no time to lose in getting everything ready.

'We'll start building our new feast hall immediately,' said Thrain. 'I need everyone in the village to help. Spread the word: King Leif the Very Uptight will be on Bear Island by next Thorsday and I will be hosting a feast in his honour.'

Hack and Whack had never been so excited in their lives. A real live king was coming to their island. And, of course, bringing gifts for everyone, because Viking kings were famous for their generosity.

Hack dreamed of her new

sword, with a decorated hilt covered in jewels.

Whack dreamed of his new axe, engraved with gold.

Twisty Pants dreamed of his magic amulet.

Dirty Ulf hoped for a new board game.

Elsa Gold-Hair imagined her new silver brooch.

No one could talk about anything else.

'So exciting,' said Mum. 'Bear Island's first royal feast.'

'But not just any feast,' said Grim Grit-Teeth. 'A **three-day** feast.'

'The biggest feast ever held on Bear Island,' said Dad.

'I'm not going if I have to have a bath,' muttered Dirty Ulf.

'There will be drinking contests and song singing and poetry reciting,' said Hildi Horn-Head.

'And lots and lots of food!' shouted Bragi Bread-Nose. 'Roast pork. Roast lamb. Spit-roasted venison and beef.'

'Yummy!' shouted Hack. Wow, what a treat. Her tummy was already rumbling.

'And no whale blubber!' shouted

Whack.

'And barrels of mead
and beer to toast
Odin and King Leif the
Very Uptight,' cheered Kari
Snooze.

'Not to mention food fights
and whacking each other with
leeks, and ale drinking until
everyone gets drunk and throws
up and starts brawling,' said
Grimolf the Fearless,
whooping.

Wow, thought Whack. That sounds brilliant.

'And we're invited to the best feast ever,' said Hack, swinging her sword and doing a happy dance.

'Yippee!' said Whack, jumping up and down.

'No, you're not,' said Dad.

Hack stopped dancing.

'No children,' said Mum.

Whack stopped jumping.

'What?' said Hack. 'What about

my new sword from the king?'

'What?' said Whack. 'What about my new axe?

'Children are not welcome at royal feasts,' said Dad.

'NOOOOOOOOOO!' screamed Hack.

'NOOOOOOOOOO!' screamed Whack.

The village rang with the sounds of hammering and pounding as the new timber-framed feast hall rose from the ground.

Hack, Whack, Twisty Pants and Elsa Gold-Hair met in the forest, where they'd been sent to gather wood to line the new roasting pits.

'I'll die if I have to carry any more wood,' moaned Whack.

'Me too,' agreed Hack.

'It's so unfair. We have to

work and we're not even invited to the feast,' said Whack.

'We're going,' said Hack.

'Not if we're not invited,' said Elsa Gold-Hair.

'Of course we are,' said Hack. 'And if we get into trouble we'll steal some horses and escape.'

'Yeah,' said Whack. 'I'm not missing a food-fight ... and I want my axe from the king.'

'Of course **I've** met the king,' boasted Twisty Pants.

The two terrible Vikings stared at Twisty Pants.

'You've met the king?' said Hack. 'The actual king?'

'What was he like?' gasped Whack.

'Did you bow?' asked Hack.

'Nah,' said Twisty Pants. 'In fact, the king bowed to **me**, and said, "All hail, great Twisty Pants".'

'And then what?' said Whack.

'I said, "Howdy, King. How's it going, big guy? Nice crown. Gimme some gold".'

'Is **that** the right way to greet a king?' said Hack.

'Yeah — if you're friends,' said Twisty Pants.

'But what happens if you address him the wrong way?' asked Elsa Gold-Hair.

'He chops off your head,' said Twisty Pants. 'When I met him the first time I forgot the correct greeting, but he let me recite a poem as ransom for my head, so here I am.'

'Really?' said Whack. Sometimes he had the feeling that Twisty Pants made things up.

'Really,' said Twisty Pants.

'What did you recite?' said Elsa Gold-Hair.

'Oh,' bragged Twisty Pants, 'just a fantastic poem about how my head looked so good on my shoulders it would be a shame to chop it off. And a few extra verses about what a great king he was.'

'Yoo-hoo!' bellowed Dirty Ulf, skipping over with a basket of wild leeks. 'I've got great news,' she said. 'Thrain Scatter-Brain says that **everyone** on Bear Island is invited to his feast for the king. Including us.'

'I'll get my sword!' shrieked Hack.

'Food-fights, here we come!' shrieked Whack.

The terrible Vikings whooped and hollered and ran home to tell Mum the great news.

'We're going to the feast,' sang Hack and Whack. 'We're going to the feee-east.'

'What did you say?' whispered Mum. She looked like she was going to faint.

'We're invited to the feast,' said Hack.

'We're going to feast with the king!' said Whack.

'Ouch!' Whack straightened up and rubbed his back. 'I hate weeding. What's the point?'

Hack and Whack were weeding the vegetable garden next to their longhouse.

'The king won't care if he sees a weed with the beans,' said Whack.

'How do you know?' said Hack. 'He'll probably walk through the village and inspect everything and everyone.'

'I wish it was feast day already,' said Whack.

Twisty Pants strolled by, muttering to himself.

'Yoo-hoo! Twisty Pants, get over here,' shouted Hack. 'Help us or we'll never finish weeding.'

Twisty Pants stopped muttering. 'You've made me lose my train of thought. I'm composing a poem for the king.'

Hack stopped hoeing.

'Let's hear it.'

Twisty Pants struck a pose.

'Oh Great King Leif the Very Very
Very Uptight,
When I heard you were coming I
jumped with delight.
I'm sad I'm too young to sail off
and fight.
But until I can pillage
every village,
And bring **you** loads of treasure,
Give me a gold ring (or two, or
five),

And an armband, and a silver
brooch,
And a sword and an axe,
And a horse and a shield,
And a magic amulet,
And I'll sing your praises, day
and night.'

'He's sure to reward me handsomely for my great poem,' bragged Twisty Pants.

That's a **terrible** poem, thought Whack.

'I can recite a much better poem,' said Hack.

'Oh yeah?' said Twisty Pants.

'Yeah,' said Hack.

'Hand over some loot
Or I'll give you the boot.'

'Short and snappy,' said Hack, preening.

'You can't order the king to give you gifts,' said Elsa Gold-Hair, walking past with baskets of nuts. Dirty Ulf followed her, carrying baskets of strawberries.

'Why not?' said Whack. 'I want ... gets.'

'But what if **I** want what **you** want?' said Elsa.

'Tough,' said Whack. 'I didn't say, "**You** want ... you get". It's "I want ... I get".' That's the Viking rule.'

Elsa Gold-Hair decided not to argue.

'My dad says that everyone will have to stand before King Leif and recite their greatest deeds,' said Elsa Gold-Hair.

'Don't mention sharing,' said Hack.

'Oh,' said Elsa. That was

exactly her plan. 'Then I'll say how I screamed and scared Grunt Iron-Skull.'

'Good thing the feast will last for three days because that's how long it will take for **me** to recite my greatest deeds,' boasted Twisty Pants.

'Whack and I are the worst Vikings in the village,' said Hack, twirling her sword. 'That's our greatest deed.'

'I've gone for a year without

combing my hair,' said Dirty Ulf, swinging her tangled mop of curls proudly.

'That's not a great deed,' said Elsa.

'It is if you know my mother,' said Dirty Ulf.

It was the day before the royal feast. Chieftain Thrain Scatter-Brain had called a village meeting at the new hall.

Everyone gathered inside and sat at the shiny new tables on the shiny new benches. The hall smelled of fresh straw and peat. The long tables were laid with wooden platters, drinking horns and spoons. All the children were seated on the lowest benches, furthest away from the king's high seat.

Thrain Scatter-Brain called everyone to attention. 'King Leif the Very Uptight arrives tomorrow,' he said. 'Who knows the rules for feasting with a king?'

The hall was silent.

'That's what I was afraid of,' said Thrain. 'We all need to learn proper behaviour when feasting with a king. Especially a king like King Leif the Very Uptight.

He insists on correct manners in his presence. I warn you that he's even more extreme than his father King Leif the Uptight. And you all know how strict **he** was.'

The hall hushed.

'I'm the only Viking here who has visited a king's court, so I know all the rules about how to act around royalty.'

'Does this mean no drinking until you're so drunk you throw

up over everyone?' said Gapi
the Baldy.

'No getting drunk and
vomiting,' said Thrain Scatter-
Brain, shuddering. 'This is a
royal feast with the strictest
Viking king who has ever lived.'

'What about bone throwing?'
said Glumra Bug-Bear.

'NO bone throwing,' said
Thrain Scatter-Brain.

'I heard that the last time
someone threw food at a royal

feast, King Leif had him locked in a haunted privy for a week,' said Erik Gold-Hair.

'But how can you have a feast without throwing bones?' said Whack.

'Shh,' said Elsa Gold-Hair.

'. . . You also need to know which spoon to use,' said the chieftain. 'You can't just grab the food. Once King Leif saw someone use the wrong spoon and banished him to Sheep Island. We need to practise our manners,' added Thrain. 'We

will now all pretend we are at the royal feast.'

Servants brought out platters of bread and pitchers of ale. Thrain walked around the benches.

'Pass the drinking horn to the person on your left, not on your right, Gapi the Baldy! Hegg the Hungry once passed the drinking horn to the right instead of to the left in front of King Leif. Hegg has never been seen again.'

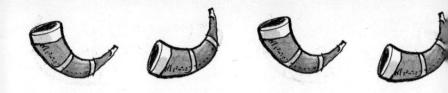

Yikes, thought Hack. This feast sounded ... awful.

'I'm not going,' said Whack. Gutting fish and weeding the vegetable patch suddenly seemed like a lot more fun.

'Sneeze into the water bowl, not into your sleeve, Kari Snooze,' said Thrain. 'No hogging the drinking horn, Bragi Bread-Nose. Don't drink it all at once, Olga Fish-Belly.

Remember, you will each be sharing your drinking horn with one of the king's men.'

Everyone started shouting and roaring.

'What do you mean **share** a drinking horn?' bellowed Sven Fork-Beard. 'We're Vikings, and Vikings **never** share!'

'Except drinking horns,' said Thrain Scatter-Brain. 'Do you want the king to think we're

barbarians? It's good manners and a sign of friendship to share a horn. Elbows **off** the table, Hack and Whack. Don't chew with your mouth open, Twisty Pants. Wipe your hands on your bread, not on your cloak, Dirty Ulf. Eat with your spoon, not your fingers, Black Tooth. Children will sit still and not speak unless spoken to.'

'For three days?' said Hack.

'So many rules,' said Dirty Ulf.

Another servant brought round a hot water bowl.

'Stop! Stop, Grim Grit-Teeth!' shrieked Thrain. 'When the hot water bowl is passed round, wash your hands and face and **then** spit in it before passing it to your neighbour. And Sven Fork-Beard,' yelled Thrain, 'how many times do I have to remind you? Blow your nose **into** the water bowl, not on your hands.'

Elsa Gold-Hair couldn't

believe her ears. A feast where everyone ate with their spoons, sat up straight, didn't throw bones, and no one got drunk? She couldn't wait!

Hack and Whack couldn't believe their ears. A feast where no one ate with their fingers, or threw food, or got drunk? And they couldn't speak unless spoken to? This sounded like the most boring feast ever.

'I'm not going,' said Hack.

'Me neither,' said Whack.

'You **have** to go,' said Mum.

'But the feast lasts for three days,' wailed Whack.

'I can't remember all those stupid rules,' wailed Hack.

Mum and Dad stuffed Hack and Whack, kicking and screaming, into their best cloaks and tunics. Hack felt like a trussed-up sausage in her best pinafore dress and woollen cloak. Whack squeezed into his best leggings, which were too tight. Bitey-Bitey looked as miserable as Hack and Whack. Even he had been forced to have a bath. Hack and Whack didn't recognise Dirty Ulf, she was so scrubbed.

Everyone gathered in the new feast hall and waited. And waited. And waited.

Finally, a cry went up.

'The king's dragon-headed longship is in the harbour! The king is coming! The king is coming!'

The hall hushed. Everyone sat up straight and tried to remember all the rules for feasting with royalty.

Do I pass the drinking horn to the left or to the right? thought Hack miserably.

Do I sneeze in my sleeve or in the washing water? thought Whack miserably.

Would the king see them slouching or using the wrong spoon and banish them to Greenland?

'Make way for King Leif!' boomed a voice from outside. Then a teenage boy strode into the room, surrounded by armed men, berserker warriors and

dogs. He raced between the tables to the raised dais and hurled himself into the high seat.

'Where's King Leif the Very Uptight?' asked Thrain.

'Dead,' said the boy, grabbing a drinking horn and swallowing the mead in one long gulp. 'I'm

the new king — his son Leif
the Rowdy. And I'm here to ...
PARTY!'

There was a shocked silence.

'Does that mean I can use any
spoon?' whispered Elsa Gold-
Hair.

'Come on! Is this a funeral
or a feast?' bellowed the king,
leaping on to a table, grabbing
several chicken legs and hurling
them at Thrain.

Hack and Whack didn't wait

to be asked twice.

'FOOD-FIGHT!' they shrieked, leaping onto the table and hurling food at Kari Snooze.

'PARTY!' shrieked Dirty Ulf and Twisty Pants, hurling bread and a plateful of leeks at Sven Fork-Beard.

'DRINK UP, everyone,' shouted Leif the Rowdy. He picked up a barrel of ale and poured it over his warriors. 'We're going to feast till we drop!'

Hack admired her shining new sword.

Whack admired his gleaming new axe.

Dirty Ulf admired her ivory chess pieces.

Twisty Pants admired his Thor amulet.

Elsa Gold-Hair admired her new brooch.

Bitey-Bitey bounced home with his new bone.

King Leif the Rowdy had been **very** generous with his gifts. And his praise. 'Hack and Whack are the best worst Vikings ever!' he'd shouted, before falling asleep under the table.

'Wow,' said Hack, as the family staggered home covered in food and ale. 'That was the best feast EVER.'

'And we get to do it all over again tomorrow,' cheered Whack. 'Long live King Leif the Rowdy!'

HACK AND WHACK AND THE WINTER GUESTS WHO WON'T LEAVE

KNOCK! KNOCK! KNOCK! KNOCK! KNOCK!

'We're here!' boomed a voice outside the door. 'Helloooooo!

Anybody home?'

Mum wiped her cold, fish-scale-covered hands on her apron. Hack stopped stirring the cauldron of soup suspended over the fire. Whack stopped striking sparks on his flint. Dad put down the fishing net he was mending and reached for his axe.

'Who's there?' said Mum.

'It's your cousin, Ketil Flat-Nose!'

'What in Thor's name is Cousin Ketil doing here so far from his home?' hissed Mum. She looked around the longhouse – there were fishing nets piled on the floor, and fish drying everywhere. '**And** in winter? No one travels in winter.'

'Who's Cousin Ketil Flat-Nose?' hissed Hack.

'You know – filthy-rich Cousin Ketil,' hissed Dad, kicking aside the tangled nets. 'The one who made a fortune bringing wheat and honey and cloth from England.'

'Raiding, not trading,' said Mum, smoothing her hair.

'Ooh,' said Whack. 'Can Cousin Ketil take me raiding next summer so I can get rich too?'

'And me,' said Hack.

'His raiding days are over,' said Dad. 'He's too old now.'

BANG! BANG! BANG! BANG! BANG!

'Open up — we're freezing!' shouted Ketil Flat-Nose.

Dad opened the door to a blast of sleet and howling wind. Two people huddled in snow-covered furs hurried inside and stood by the hearth, dripping water and slush, stamping their hairy boots and clapping their gloved

hands. A fat, wet dog waddled in after them and stretched out in front of the smoking fire, blocking the heat.

'Is my little coochie-poochie warmer now?' trilled a sulky voice from inside one of the fur hoods. The teenage girl's twisted gold bracelets clanked as she kneeled to pet the panting dog. Then she looked at Hack and Whack, and scowled. 'Hey, you! Build up that fire! I'm freezing! And where's my hot water and fresh towels? Is this how you greet a guest?'

Dad ran to get extra wood from the woodpile. Mum dashed off to find towels and heat some water on the fire. Hack and Whack stood still, for maybe the first time ever. They stared at their unexpected guests. Ketil Flat-Nose was wearing a fur-trimmed hat on top of his sparse white hair and his right arm hung stiffly by his side. A gold brooch fastened his fur-lined cloak over his tunic, which was embroidered with gold and silver thread and had silk-lined sleeves. His belt buckle was silver and he wore billowing green trousers bound with leather straps below the knees. He looked like a walking treasure chest.

'Aren't you expecting us?' said Ketil, holding his chapped

hands closer to the fire. 'I sent people ahead to warn you.'

Whack bit his lip. So **that's** what those strangers who stopped by yesterday were babbling about. He'd completely forgotten to pass on the message to Mum and Dad.

Oh well.

'How long can you stay?' said Mum. If they leave in three days there will be no problem with food, she thought.

'Don't worry, my daughter Gudrun Grim-Tongue and I are here for the whole winter!' boomed Cousin Ketil. 'It's been ages since we've had a nice long visit.'

Mum gulped. The **whole** winter? Her eyes flicked to the half-empty barrels of salted fish and pork in the storeroom.

'There was a **little** trouble back home so we thought we'd come here,' said Ketil. He lowered his voice and whispered. Hack heard the words 'Gudrun' and 'unsuitable boy', and 'fortune hunter'.

Gudrun Grim-Tongue gazed around the longhouse and pulled her bear-skin cloak tighter around her silk dress.

'Why are we standing here in the servants' hovel?' she snapped. 'It stinks. And speaking of servants, where in Thor's name are they? I want a hot bath. Tell those lazy lumps to get in here and make it snappy.'

Hack looked at Whack. What was Cousin Gudrun on about?

'We don't have any servants,' said Whack.

Gudrun Grim-Tongue stared. 'That's impossible. Who feeds the animals and does the cooking and cleans the stables?'

'We do,' said Hack.

Gudrun Grim-Tongue gasped. 'You're joking?'

'Don't be rude, Gudrun,' said her father, limping to the table and sitting on the bench. 'Not everyone has servants and farms and gold and silver like us.'

'But why are we staying with **poor** relations?' wailed Gudrun. 'They don't even have cushions or wall hangings!'

Mum returned and handed

round bowls of hot water for the winter guests and offered them each a towel.

'Where's my bed closet?' said Gudrun Grim-Tongue. 'I want to rest.'

'We all sleep in this room,' said Dad. 'But don't worry, Hack and Whack can sleep on the floor or with the cows, and you can have their sleep-bench.'

'You expect me to sleep ... in here?' screeched Gudrun.

'With ... everyone? Like a ... a pig?'

'How long is she staying?' muttered Hack.

'The winter,' said Mum.

Hack thought she must have misheard.

'You mean till Wodensday.'

'No, the winter.'

'The **whole** winter?' said Whack.

'Yes,' said Mum. She looked grim. 'But I'm sure Gudrun will

be a great help with all the chores and—'

STOMP! STOMP! STOMP!

The ground shuddered and every shield and sword hanging on the longhouse walls shook.

'What's that noise?' said Gudrun.

'That's the berserker next door, Grunt Iron-Skull,' said Hack. 'He's back again from the wars.'

'He likes stomping around scaring everyone,' said Whack.

'Except us,' said Hack.

''Cause we're the worst Vikings in the village!' they shrieked.

Gudrun covered her ears.

'Don't speak to him, or even **look** at him, Gudrun,' ordered her father. 'Berserkers are bad news.'

'A berserker is the **least** of my problems, Dad,' whined Gudrun Grim-Tongue. 'Why didn't you tell me we were going to stay in a pigsty with two loudmouths? You know I hate children. You know I need peace and quiet.'

Hack looked at Whack.

Whack looked at Hack.

It was going to be a long winter.

Ow! Whack sat up and rubbed his side. He missed his sleep-bench. Sleeping on the dirt floor was horrible.

Ow! Hack sat up and rubbed her neck. She missed her sleep-bench. Sleeping on the dirt floor was horrible.

SNORE! SNORE! SNORE!

Gudrun Grim-Tongue snored louder than a troll.

'She should be sleeping with the pigs,' said Hack.

'Yeah,' said Whack. 'She'd fit right in.'

'I heard that, stink-breath,' snapped Gudrun, opening her eyes.

Mum bustled in, wiping bread dough off her hands.

'Gudrun, you're awake,' she said. 'I'm so pleased to have an extra pair of hands. I could really use some help with the weaving today.'

Gudrun stared. 'Weave?' she said. 'I don't weave.'

'Brew ale?' said Mum.

'What?' said Gudrun.

'Make sour-milk cheese?'

'Are you joking?' said Gudrun.

'Gut fish?' asked Mum faintly.

'My servants do all that,' said Gudrun. 'I have better things to do,' she added, yawning and admiring her clean nails. 'What I want now is a hot bath,' she ordered.

'Hack, Whack, go fetch some water,' said Mum.

It was going to be a **very** long winter.

GLUG, GLUG, GLUG. Hack dipped her bucket into the icy stream, then trudged back through the drifting snow to the longhouse, cold water slopping over her boots and leggings. It was still dark; the winter sun hadn't risen yet. Maybe today would be the day it didn't rise at all.

Whack dragged a bucket of icy water from the stream and trudged back to the longhouse.

The freezing air bit his face.

Worse, Hack and Whack knew that as soon as they'd emptied the water into the iron cauldron over the fire, they'd be sent back out into the cold to fetch more. And more. And more.

'What are we, servants?' moaned Hack.

'Worse than servants,' said Whack. 'At least servants get paid.'

'Gudrun doesn't do **any** work,' said Hack.

'She can't even pluck a chicken,' said Whack.

'When will that troll-bellied, stinky-breath, ogre-nosed hag LEAVE?' wailed Hack.

'Not until the first summer month,' said Whack.

'We won't live that long,' said Hack sadly. 'We'll be walking skeletons.'

The next night, in honour of the winter guests, Mum spit-roasted some lamb with wild garlic. Whack's mouth watered. Roast lamb! This was a rare treat. Usually they just ate salted fish or pork during winter. At least there was one good thing about Ketil Flat-Nose and Gudrun Grim-Tongue coming to visit.

Ketil Flat-Nose, sitting in the seat of honour, heaped steaming meat onto his plate. Then he passed the wooden platter to Gudrun.

'About time there was something decent to eat around here,' said Gudrun, scooping a gigantic portion of roast meat onto her plate. Then, instead of passing the platter, she took another huge helping.

'Here, coochie-poochie,' she cooed, offering thick slices of lamb to her ugly dog Garm, who was drooling by her feet under the table. 'Something for your little tum-tum. And here's a nice bone,' she added, nabbing a huge bone laden with meat and tossing it on the floor. Garm set to work, gnawing and chewing and tearing.

Hack's stomach rumbled.

Whack's stomach rumbled.

Bitey-Bitey's stomach rumbled.

'Family, hold back,' murmured Dad, taking a thin slice.

Bitey-Bitey thought he'd snatch some meat from Garm. Then he looked at Garm's frothing jaws again and slunk off, whimpering.

Hack got a sliver of gristle.

She passed the platter to Whack.

Whack got a tiny piece of fat.

'I'm hungry,' wailed Whack.

Gudrun Grim-Tongue looked up from her plate.

'Oh, have this,' she said, reaching under the table and tossing him the bone Garm had finished gnawing.

Whack looked at the lamb bone covered in drool.

Garm the fat dog got the meat and **he** got the bone? It was so unfair.

He watched as Gudrun shovelled the last of the lamb from her wooden trencher into her mouth with her fingers.

'Love a girl with a healthy appetite,' boomed Ketil, gorging on his own heaped platter of meat.

Healthy appetite? thought Hack. She eats like an ogre.

'There's too much grit in this bread,' complained Gudrun. 'Where's the wine?'

'No wine,' said Dad. 'Just ale.'

Gudrun gasped.

'You don't even have glasses,' said Gudrun. 'How can you expect me to drink from a cattle horn? And I'm still hungry,' she moaned.

'Have some whale blubber,' said Whack.

Every meal was the same. Gudrun took a huge portion of food for herself, and another huge helping for her horrible dog. By the time the food reached Hack and Whack there was barely any left.

Hack, Whack, Mum, Dad and Bitey-Bitey got thinner and thinner and thinner. Gudrun Grim-Tongue, Ketil Flat-Nose and Garm got fatter and fatter and fatter.

Something had to be done.

'I'll die if I have to carry another bucket of water,' moaned Whack. 'I'm so tired. I need my rest.'

Dirty Ulf, Elsa Gold-Hair and Twisty Pants ran over through the snow, each carrying bundles of firewood. In the distance came clanging and hammering from Dirty Ulf's father's smithy.

'What are you doing?' said Dirty Ulf. 'I've watched you lugging water up from the stream for ages.'

'It's for Gudrun Grim-Tongue's bath,' said Hack. She set down her bucket in the snow and

rubbed her aching arms. 'She takes one every single day.'

Dirty Ulf gasped. 'Every day! I thought once a year was bad enough.'

'She's used to a hot-spring bathing pool in Iceland,' said Whack. 'They have one on all their farms.'

'I wish she'd melted in one

before she ever came here,' said Hack.

'I'm NEVER moving to Iceland,' said Dirty Ulf, shuddering. She imagined the horror — bathing pools popping up all over the place? There'd be no escape from those vicious bathtubs.

'What are we going to do?' wailed Hack.

'Gudrun Grim-Tongue just sits on her big bottom while we work and work and work,' wailed

Whack. 'And she eats like a horse.'

'Make that two horses,' said Hack.

'Mum says we're running out of food,' said Whack. 'I'm always hungry.'

'How can we make her leave?' said Hack.

'You can't,' said Elsa Gold-Hair. 'Winter guests need shelter until the first summer month.'

'But that's not for **ages**,' said Whack.

'It'll be the end of days before then,' said Hack.

'Guests, like fish, stink after three days,' said Twisty Pants. 'Everyone knows that.'

'Gudrun stank after three minutes,' said Hack.

'There has to be a way to make her leave,' said Whack. 'There just has to.'

'Lucky you met me,' said Twisty Pants. 'I know how to get rid of stinky guests.'

'How?' said Whack.

'Easy,' said Twisty Pants. 'Farts.'

'Great idea, Twisty Pants,' said Dirty Ulf. 'Everyone loves the smell of their own farts, but no one likes anyone else's.'

'Ewwwwww,' said Elsa Gold-Hair.

'Yes!' said Whack. 'We can drive Gudrun and Ketil away with bad smells.'

Hack considered this. The longhouse already stank of fish oil, cow dung and smoke.

'I'm not sure farts would make the longhouse smell worse than it already does,' she said sadly.

'Then leave her bathwater cold,' said Dirty Ulf.

'Spill sour-milk cheese in her bed,' said Twisty Pants.

'Put herrings in her boots,' said Dirty Ulf.

'Tell her an undead creature

haunts your longhouse,' said Elsa Gold-Hair.

Hack's eyes gleamed.

Whack grinned.

Hack and Whack left Gudrun's bathwater cold. They put sour-milk cheese in her bed. They put herrings in her boots and told her that Ivor the Boneless haunted the longhouse.

But nothing worked. When Gudrun wasn't hogging the

bath-house and eating all the nuts, she sat by the hearth, feeding her dog, combing her hair, admiring her jewels, and screaming at them to be quiet.

And after Gudrun complained, Mum made Hack and Whack do even **more** chores for being so rude to a guest.

'I've got it,' said Whack. 'Let's get Bitey-Bitey to bite her bottom.'

Yes!

'Go on, Bitey, bite her bum,'

said Hack.

Bitey-Bitey perked up.

The wolf cub crept up to the tempting target, who was standing facing the fire. Bitey crouched and . . .

RAAAAAAAAAAA! Garm hurled himself at Bitey-Bitey.

Bitey-Bitey ran off to the cow shed.

'We **have** to do something,' said Hack, piling up firewood.

'**Anything**,' said Whack. 'My arms are going to fall off.'

'And Dad said we had to help him repair the frost damage on the home meadow wall tomorrow, on top of everything else,' said Whack.

'I have an idea,' said Hack.

'Tell me! Tell me!' said Whack.

'It's dangerous,' said Hack.

'Even better. We're the worst Vikings in the village. We live for danger.'

'Are we Vikings or whale blubber?' said Hack.

'Vikings!' shouted Whack.

'Okay, then,' said Hack. She whispered her plan to Whack.

'Let's do it,' he said. 'We're Hack and Whack, on the attack!'

Hack and Whack met Ketil Flat-Nose in the home meadow as he returned from hunting.

'The berserker Grunt Iron-Skull is walking around the village reciting love poems about Gudrun,' said Hack.

Ketil Flat-Nose went pale. 'What?' he roared. 'How dare he.'

'We thought you should know,' said Whack.

'What is he saying?' said Ketil.

'Here's one I heard,' said Hack.

'Oh lovely Gudrun,
Grimmest of Grim-Tongues,
I've broken my teeth biting my
shield.
But I'll love my sea-goddess
as long as two teeth
stick to my gums.'

Ketil's face was red with fury.
'How dare he use my daughter's
name in his verses. What an insult.'

'That's not all,' said Whack. 'Here's his latest.

Oh Gudrun,

When I see you waddling about,

My love for you is never in doubt.

Goddess laden with silver and gold,

Seeing your rich jewels makes

me bold.

Can't wait to get my hands on all

your money.

Thank you for your love-words

dripping with honey.'

'Where did you hear that?'
gasped Ketil.

'Grunt's verses about Gudrun
are all over the village,' said Hack.

Ketil Flat-Nose scowled. 'How

dare he insult her,' he snarled.

'**She's** reciting verses too,' said Hack.

'What?' gasped Ketil.

'They must be in love,' said Whack. 'Here's what Gudrun has been saying.

Oh Grunt, my darling lump,
Bravest of beasts that go bump.
Even Odin runs away
When Grunty joins the battle fray.
Every giant flees the fight

When Grunt throws spears with
all his might.
You make my heart go thumpety-
thump,
My very own Grunty Grunt.'

Ketil staggered and sat down on the wall. Gudrun in love . . . with a berserker? Impossible.

And yet . . . hadn't they come to Bear Island to get Gudrun away from **another** terrible suitor?

'Grunt Iron-Skull is insulting my daughter **and** insulting me with his verses and I won't allow it,' growled Ketil, limping over to Grunt Iron-Skull's longhouse and pounding on the studded door.

'Open up, Grunt Iron-Skull, you

dribbling, pot-licking pile of rotting fish. I want a word with you!'

Grunt Iron-Skull flung open the door. He towered over Ketil Flat-Nose. His hel-hound Muddy Butt snarled.

'Oh yeah?' growled Grunt.

'Yeah,' said Ketil.

Hack and Whack never discovered what Grunt said to Ketil. But all they knew was that Gudrun Grim-Tongue and Ketil

Even-Flatter-Nose   left   Bear Island that night.

'We've been your winter guests long enough,' said Ketil Even-Flatter-Nose, rushing out the door as fast as his battle-scarred leg could carry him. 'We're off to visit Thorir Long-Chin on Seal Island. Come along, Gudrun. The boat's all ready.'

'But why?' whined Gudrun, as they hurried into the darkness towards the harbour.

'You know why,' snapped Ketil.

Inside the suddenly peaceful longhouse, the hearth fire crackled. A pot of stew boiled. Bitey-Bitey stretched out in front of the fire and sighed, taking the warm spot Garm had hogged.

Mum looked at Dad.

Dad looked at Mum.

'Well,' said Mum.

'Well,' said Dad.

'Was this your doing, Hack and Whack?' said Mum.

'No,' lied Hack.

'No,' lied Whack.

'Let's see what I've got in the storeroom,' said Mum. 'I think my best worst Vikings have earned a family feast!'